Mangroves

Heather Hammonds

Contents

Mangroves

What Are Mangroves?

Mangroves are a special group of plants that live around water. They grow in muddy, salty places close to the seashore. Mangrove forests can be found beside bays and **inlets**. They are also found at places where rivers flow into the sea, called estuaries (say: *es-choo-a-rees*).

Mangroves grow in the "intertidal zone". This is the name for the area of land that is covered with water when the tide comes in. It is uncovered when the tide goes out.

Mangrove plants have big roots that grow in water.

Mangrove forests are home to thousands of different animals. Small creatures live in the water around mangrove roots. Birds and other animals live among the trees and shrubs, too.

Water birds are some of the animals that live near mangroves.

Mangrove forests grow in warmer parts of the world. They do not grow in places where it is frosty or very cold.

How Mangroves Live and Grow

Different kinds of mangrove trees and shrubs grow in mangrove forests. All mangroves are able to survive in a salty environment.

There are very tall mangroves that grow into huge trees and smaller mangroves that grow lower to the ground.

Some mangroves have strong roots that grow above the ground.

Other mangroves have very wide roots that grow along the ground.

The roots help the mangroves to stay in place when water washes around them as the tide goes in and out.

This mangrove has wide roots.

Wet soil in mangrove forests has very little **oxygen** in it to help plants grow. Some mangroves have small "breathing roots" that help them to get oxygen.

The breathing roots of this mangrove are sticking out of the water.

Many plants cannot survive in places where there is lots of salt. Salty water and salty ground are very harmful to them.

However, mangrove trees and shrubs have several different ways of preventing salt from damaging them.

Some mangroves get rid of salt through tiny openings in their leaves.

This mangrove is getting rid of salt through its leaves.

Other mangroves store salt inside their bark and leaves. Over time, the bark and leaves grow old and fall off, and the mangroves get rid of the salt.

Old, dead leaves have fallen off this mangrove.

Some mangroves also have roots that can **filter** out most of the salt and stop it from getting inside the plant.

Mangroves and Wildlife

Animals of all sizes live in mangrove forests.

Fish

Mangrove forests are a good place for fish **nurseries**. Baby fish live in the water around mangrove roots. The roots help keep them safe from predators while they grow. It is hard for larger predators to swim through the roots and find the little fish.

The time baby fish spend in the mangroves is an important part of their life cycle.

Baby fish are safe living in mangrove roots.

In the mangroves, little fish feed on rotting leaves and other plant material. They eat tiny insects, too.

When some young fish that live in the water of mangrove forests grow larger, they swim away into the sea.

The mangrove jack (also called mangrove red snapper) lives safely in the water of mangrove forests until it is big enough to swim out to sea.

Fish feed on plant material in the water around mangroves.

Other Animals

Other animals live in mangrove forests, too. Thousands of crabs live in the water and mud around the mangroves.

These crabs live around a mangrove forest in Indonesia.

Water birds catch fish in the shallow water around the mangroves and build their nests in the trees and shrubs.

There are a lot of fish around the mangroves for this heron to eat.

Crocodiles and alligators make their homes in some mangrove forests. These reptiles are found in the **tropical** areas of many countries where mangroves grow. Other reptiles, such as snakes, live in some mangrove forests, too.

A crocodile rests among mangroves in a tropical part of Australia.

Mangroves and Erosion

Mangroves help stop **erosion**. When there is a lot of rain, rainwater flows into rivers. Sometimes the land floods and soil is washed away.

This riverbank has been washed away.

Big waves sometimes wash onto beaches during storms, too. They wash away parts of the seashore, taking soil and sand into the sea.

Mangroves protect beaches from being washed away.

Mangrove forests help stop the land from being washed away into rivers and seas during very wet weather.

The mangroves have strong roots that help keep the soil in place when river water flows around the roots, or when stormy waves hit the beach.

Mangrove roots help filter out **pollution** from water that runs off the land and into the sea.

Living Alongside Mangroves

Lots of people around the world live in or near mangrove forests. They rely on the mangrove forests to help them in their daily lives.

Some people live in mangrove forests in houses built from mangrove wood.

People use the wood from mangrove trees to build houses, canoes and wooden products, such as furniture.

Baskets and brown **dyes** can also be made from parts of mangrove plants.

Parts of a mangrove plant can be used to make a basket.

Some mangroves have fruits that are not safe to eat. However, others have delicious fruits that are eaten by many people who live around mangrove forests.

The mangrove apple is a popular fruit in some countries. Leaves from the mangrove apple tree can also be eaten.

People also eat the many fish and shellfish that live and grow in the water around mangroves.

People who live around mangrove forests catch fish for food.

Mangrove Forests Under Threat

Today, many mangrove forests around the world are under threat.

Every year, large areas of mangrove forests are cleared. The land is then used to build houses and factories.

Huge numbers of mangrove trees are chopped down for their wood. Mangrove forests are also cleared to build prawn and shrimp farms.

This area used to be a mangrove forest.

Large amounts of pollution, such as **pesticides** from drains and farmland, are also harming mangrove forests. The pollution can kill the plants and animals that live in the forests.

Sometimes, people also dump rubbish in the mangrove forests.

Rubbish is very harmful to animals living in mangrove forests.

As Earth's climate warms, sea levels rise. This is a threat to mangrove forests.

Mangrove forests are a very important part of the environment.

Without mangroves, thousands of animals would not have food or shelter. People would not have wood, fruit or fish from the forests. Land would be washed away in some places during storms.

It is important to protect the mangrove forests of the world.

A mangrove forest is a beautiful sight from above.

Save Our Mangrove Forest!

Dear Mayor Johnson,

We have read of plans to turn the mangrove forest near our school into a **marina**, for boats. We believe that the mangrove forest should not be destroyed!

First, thousands of small animals live in the water around the mangroves. We have seen fish and shellfish, such as crabs, whenever we visit the forest. Baby fish swim safely among the mangrove roots.

Second, birds build their nests in the mangrove trees. They find food for themselves and their babies in the trees and in the water. Thousands of insects also live in the forest. Snakes slither among the mangroves, too.

Third, the mangrove forest grows beside the bay.
On stormy days, there are high tides and big waves.
The roots of the mangrove trees help to stop
the soil by the bay being washed away by the waves.

Finally, our class enjoys a bushwalk through the mangrove forest every week. We learn about the plants and animals in the forest. We pick up any rubbish we find.

We believe that the mangrove forest is much more important to our environment than a boat marina!

From Grade 4,
Sandy Bay Primary School

Glossary

dyes (*noun*) liquids that can be used to change the colour of cloth or other materials

erosion (*noun*) the wearing away or breaking down of land

filter (*verb*) to separate solids from liquids by passing the liquid through small gaps

inlets (*noun*) entrances into narrow areas of water

marina (*noun*) a place where people can park or keep their boats on the water

nurseries (*noun*) places where young animals can live and grow

oxygen (*noun*) the gas in Earth's air that helps keep living things alive

pesticides (*noun*) substances that are made to kill insects and other living things

pollution (*noun*) poisonous or dangerous substances put in the environment

tropical (*adjective*) very hot but not dry; often rainy or steamy

Index